Wake Up, Color Pup

For Alison

All rights reserved. Published in the United States by Random House Children's Books,

a division of Penguin Random House LLC, New York.

Random House and the colophon are registered trademarks of Penguin Random House LLC.

Visit us on the Web! rhcbooks.com

Educators and librarians, for a variety of teaching tools,

visit us at RHTeachersLibrarians.com

Library of Congress Cataloging-in-Publication Data is available upon request.

ISBN 978-0-399-55945-7 (trade) — ISBN 978-0-399-55946-4 (lib. bdg.) — ISBN 978-0-399-55947-1 (ebook)

Book design by Sarah Hokanson

MANUFACTURED IN CHINA

10 9 8 7 6 5 4 3 2 1   First Edition

Wake Up,
Color Pup

Taia Morley

Random House 🏠 New York

Wake up,

little pup.

Out we go!

YELLOW

Flutter,
leap, lunge.

ORANGE

Jump,

bound,

race ahead!

Trot, greet,

circle.

PURPLE

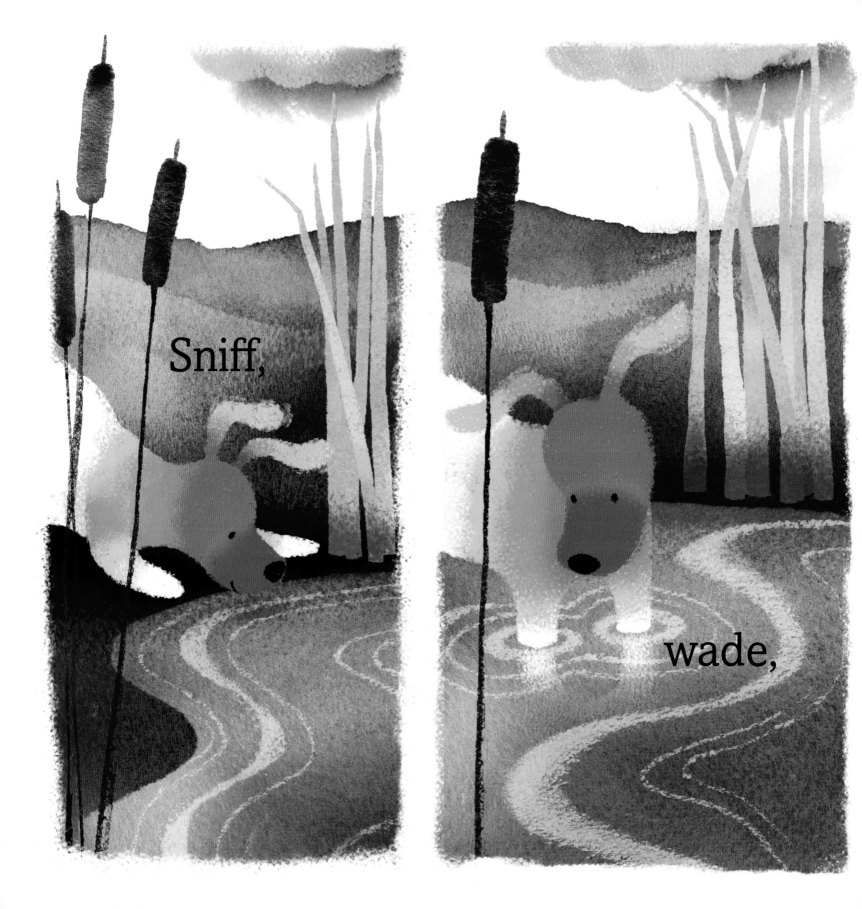

splash through. **BLUE**

Squiggle,
wiggle,

squirm
between.

GREEN

Drip,

drop,

DARK

Shiver, huddle,

stay.

GRAY

Whisper,
nudge.
Look!

PLAY!

Shimmy,

shake.

World
awake!

Ramble,
roam.
Amble
home.